The Story of the
Root Children

Originally published in German in 1906 as *Etwas von den Wurzelkindern*
English version © Floris Books, Edinburgh 1990
This edition first published in 1997. Ninth printing 2018
British Library CIP data available
ISBN 978-086315-248-1
Printed in Malaysia

The Story of the
Root Children

Sibylle von Olfers

Under the ground, deep in the earth among the roots of the trees, the little root children were fast asleep all winter long. They didn't feel the biting wind, the cold snow or the stinging hailstorms. They slept peacefully in their warm burrows. They were dreaming wonderful dreams, of the sunshine in which they had played all through the summer.

When at last winter came to an end, and the sun began to melt the snow, Mother Earth came along with her candle to wake them up.

"Wake up, children," she called kindly. "Time to get up now. You've slept long enough. Spring is coming and there's work to be done. I've brought you scissors, needles and thread, and pieces of cloth so that you can all make new clothes. Wake up! As soon as you're ready, I'll unlock and open the doors up to the ground."

The children yawned and stretched. Then they jumped up merrily. Hurray, spring is coming!

Mother Earth had pieces of lovely coloured cloth in her basket. Each of the root children chose her own colour to make a dress.
The snowdrop chose a snow-white cloth, the forget-me-not a sky-blue piece, the buttercup bright yellow, the daisy white with yellow and a bit of red, and the poppy a bright red.
Then they sat down in a cosy circle and began to work busily. They cut, sewed and pressed until everything fitted perfectly.
And as they worked, they sang all the spring songs that they knew.

As soon as they had finished making their new dresses, they went up to Mother Earth in a long procession. Mother Earth looked over her glasses in surprise when she saw the root children coming so soon.

"Well, well, you have been quick," she exclaimed, "and how nice it all looks!"

Even the little ants who had been helping Mother Earth to wind up her wool came to look inquisitively. They had never seen such splendid clothes.

But there was still more to be done. The ladybirds, the beetles, the grubs and the bumblebees had also been sleeping under the ground and had now woken up. They had to be washed and brushed, painted colourfully and made to shine so that they would look as beautiful as possible. What a hustle and bustle was going on down there!

Up above ground, the warm sun was already bringing out the new green leaves on the trees. Would the root children be ready in time?

At last it was springtime! Mother Earth opened the door and out into the warm sunshine came a procession of beetles, ladybirds and root children.

In the wood, the butterflies fluttered happily around the flowers. The lilies-of-the-valley found a cool spot in the shade of the trees beside the blue violet, and let their flower bells tinkle.

Old father Sliffslaff-Slibberslak came slowly creeping along.

"Ah-ha, there you all are! Welcome to the big forest," he said to the children.

The little violet looked at him shyly from her safe place behind her tree. She had never seen a creature like him before!

Summer came. In the little brook that flowed between the meadows, the water lily floated on the water like a princess.

The reeds whispered in the wind. The forget-me-nots came and stepped carefully into the water.

But the water beetles grumbled, "It's getting too crowded here. Go and play somewhere else!"

In the flower meadows, the root children were having lots of fun. They danced lightly in the warm sunshine. Hop and skip, whoo! If only it could always be summer!

The butterflies fluttered above them, and even the beetle had a little dance. The crickets chirped, and the bees buzzed, making wonderful music together.

"Careful, little grass, don't fall over!"

But, of course, summer came to an end. The sharp autumn wind whirled the brightly coloured leaves through the air, and tugged at the root children's clothes.

"Hooo," called the wind. "Hurry home, it's getting cold. It's time for bed."

So they all went back underground, in a long procession. Mother Earth was standing by the door and hugged each child one by one.

"Come in, children," she said, "and you too, beetles and bees. It's warm and cosy in here and I've got something for you to eat and drink. After that it's time for sleep, until I wake you up again in the springtime."

And all the little root children went down under the ground, to start their long winter's sleep.

Sibylle von Olfers' (1881–1916) blend of natural observation and simple design has led to comparisons with Kate Greenaway and Elsa Beskow.

She was born the third of five children in a castle in East Prussia. Encouraged by her aunt, she trained at art college. Her beauty attracted many admirers and suitors, but she remained aloof and distant from the "useless world of the aristocrats".

At the age of twenty-five she joined the Sisters of Saint Elizabeth, an order of nuns. As well as teaching art in the local school, she wrote and illustrated a number of children's books. Tragically, she died at the age of thirty-four from a lung infection.

My First
ROOT CHILDREN
Sibylle von Olfers

My First
SNOW CHILDREN
Sibylle von Olfers

The Story of the
RABBIT CHILDREN
Sibylle von Olfers

The
Story of the
Wind Children
Sibylle von Olfers

The Story of the
Root Children
Sibylle von Olfers

The Story of
Little Billy Bluesocks
Sibylle von Olfers

The Story of the Snow Children
Sibylle von Olfers

The Princess in the Forest
Sibylle von Olfers

The Story of
King Lion
Sibylle von Olfers

The
Story of the
Butterfly Children
Sibylle von Olfers